EASY
CAR

Carbone, Courtney

Bouncing berry hunt!

Bouncing Berry Hunt!

Adapted by **Courtney Carbone**

Based on the episode "Stop Dragon Me Around!" by **Kevin Del Aguila**

Illustrated by **Steph Lew**

A Random House PICTUREBACK® Book

Random House 🏠 New York

rhcbooks.com
ISBN 978-0-525-57787-4
Printed in the United States of America
10 9 8 7 6 5 4 3 2 1

"It's time for the Royal Scavenger Hunt!" Nella announced.

"Scavenger hunts are fun!" said Sir Garrett.

"Very fun!" Olivia added. "And not to brag, but I usually win them."

Queen Mom handed out some cards. Listed on each were four items: a metal key, a tennis racket, a red feather, and a bouncy berry. "The first team to collect all the items on the list is the winner!" she said.

Queen Mom divided the friends into three teams: Nella and Trinket, Sir Garrett and Clod, and Olivia and Smelgly.

"This dragon is not my kind of friend," Olivia told Nella. "She's clumsy and loud. . . ."

"Give her a chance, Olivia," Nella replied. "You might have more in common than you think!"

Olivia wasn't sure she agreed, but before she could say anything else, the Royal Scavenger Hunt had begun!

Nella and Trinket saw a little red bird
on a fountain. They took one of the bird's
loose feathers and put it in their basket.
They checked that item off their list.

"We found a metal key!" Sir Garrett called from the key shop. He and Clod excitedly checked the key off their list.

Now every team but Olivia and Smelgly's had found an item.

As Nella and Trinket walked away, the red feather they'd found blew out of their basket. Smelgly tried to return it to them, but Olivia stopped her.

"We need that feather, too," Olivia said. "Why don't you put it in *our* basket?"

"But that wouldn't be fair," Smelgly replied, unsure.

"If you were really my friend," Olivia said, "you would do what I ask."

Smelgly wanted to be Olivia's friend, so she agreed to keep the feather for their team.

Smelgly and Olivia went to the Learn-a-Lot Elementary School gym to look for a tennis racket. There were so many!

"One tennis racket!" Smelgly said proudly, putting it in their basket.

Olivia had an idea. "If we take them all," she said, "then the other teams can't get them!"

Smelgly didn't want to cheat, but again Olivia told her if she wanted to be a real friend, then she would help hide all the rackets. Smelgly still wasn't sure, but she did want to be Olivia's friend. She agreed to help.

Olivia and Smelgly hid the rackets in a tree. They finished just in time—Nella and Trinket were coming!

Olivia acted like her regular self. But Smelgly felt guilty, so she behaved strangely. She said hello to their friends a little too loudly and seemed nervous.

"Is it me, or is Smelgly acting kind of weird?" Trinket whispered.
"I think you're right, Trink," Nella agreed.

Olivia and Smelgly went to Willow's garden to find a bouncy berry, but they discovered that she didn't have any more! Willow had planted some new bouncy berry plants, but it would take a long time for them to grow.

"My green goo plant food makes some plants sprout really fast," Willow said. "But with bouncy berries, the green goo makes them grow huge and way too bouncy."

"Okay," Olivia said. "Thanks anyway, Willow."

As soon as Willow left, Olivia told Smelgly to pour the green goo onto the bouncy berry plants! Smelgly didn't want to cause trouble, but Olivia said she wasn't being a real friend.

So Smelgly poured the green goo onto the plants, and berries immediately began to pop out of the ground. Olivia was thrilled—until the berries grew huge and bounced toward the village!

Smelgly ran to the village as fast as she could. She found Nella and told her what had happened.

"What are you talking about?" asked Nella.

"THAT!" Smelgly cried, pointing to an avalanche of huge bouncy berries.

The bouncy berries went everywhere! Some even bounced into the tree where Smelgly and Olivia had hidden the rackets. All the rackets fell to the ground.

Nella knew just what to do! She quickly transformed into a Princess Knight, then used her bow and ribbon arrows to create a barrier to stop the bouncy berries.

"Grab a racket and bounce those berries back!" Nella called.

Everyone followed her lead and knocked the berries into a pit.

"Thanks for helping, you guys," Smelgly said, embarrassed. "I'm really sorry I made those berries grow so big and bouncy, and hid the tennis rackets in the tree—and took the red feather."

"It's not her fault," Olivia said, stepping forward. "I kept telling her I wouldn't be her friend if she didn't do everything I said. I'm sorry, Smelgly."

Nella and Trinket helped Olivia understand that being a real friend is about kindness. Olivia then told Smelgly that she hoped they could be real friends one day. Smelgly agreed and forgave Olivia.

Just then, Queen Mom arrived.
"How was the scavenger hunt?" she asked.
"Who won?"
"Somehow I think we all did!" Nella said.
Everyone cheered and celebrated by jumping into the bouncy berry ball pit they had made. Having fun together made them all feel like winners!